LIBRARY OF CONGRESS
CATALOGING-IN-PUBLICATION DATA AVAILABLE.
ISBN 978-1-4521-0620-5

BOOK DESIGN BY KRISTINE BROGNO.
TYPSET IN SACKERS GOTHIC MEDIUM.
THE ILLUSTRATIONS IN THIS BOOK WERE RENDERED
IN PENCIL DRAWINGS AND PAINTED DIGITALLY.

MANUFACTURED IN CHINA.

FSC
www.fsc.org

MIX
Paper from
responsible sources
FSC® C104723

10   9

CHRONICLE BOOKS LLC
680 SECOND STREET
SAN FRANCISCO, CALIFORNIA 94107

WWW.CHRONICLEKIDS.COM

SAN FRANCISCO, BABY!

ILLUSTRATED BY
WARD JENKINS

chronicle books · san francisco

SAN FRANCISCO WELCOMES YOU.
LET'S DO ALL THERE IS TO DO!

FIRST, LET'S **SAIL** ACROSS THE BAY
AND SEE **ALCATRAZ** ALONG THE WAY!

THEN WE'LL PASS
THE **GOLDEN GATE**.
FROM THE BOAT,
THE **VIEW** IS GREAT!

AT THE **WHARF**, WE'LL HAVE OUR LUNCH.
CRABS AND SHRIMP—
WE'LL **CRUNCH**
AND **MUNCH**!

NOW **HOP ABOARD** THE CABLE CAR.
BE SAFE—HOLD ON TO THE BAR!

IS QUITE A TREAT!

THEN WE'LL RIDE TO **UNION SQUARE**
AND DO A LITTLE SHOPPING THERE!

NEXT WE'LL GO TO **CHINATOWN**,
THROUGH **DRAGON GATE** AND ALL AROUND.

NOW I'M **HUNGRY**
AND I'M WISHIN'
TO HAVE DINNER IN
THE MISSION!

NOW IT'S LATE—THE SUN IS DOWN.
LET'S SAY **BYE-BYE** TO THIS TOWN!

OH, WHAT FUN WE'VE HAD TODAY
IN THE **CITY BY THE BAY!**